Night on 'Gator Creek

Winnie Stewart

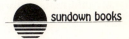
sundown books

New Readers Press ● Syracuse, New York

"TOOT, TOOT, TOOTSIE, GOODBYE" by Gus Kahn, Ernie Erdman, and Ted Fiorito ©1922, Renewed 1950 LEO FEIST INC. Rights Assigned to CBS CATALOGUE PARTNERSHIP
All Rights Controlled & Administered by CBS FEIST CATALOGUE INC.
All Rights Reserved. International Copyright Secured. Used by Permission.

ISBN 0-88336-215-5

© 1990

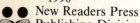 New Readers Press
Publishing Division of Laubach Literacy International
Box 131, Syracuse, New York 13210

Printed in the United States of America

Edited by Kay Koschnick
Illustrations by Pat Austin
Cover design by Chris Steenwerth
Cover photo by Dave Revette
9 8 7 6 5 4 3 2

To Willie and R.W.

Chapter 1

When Gram and Gramps showed up at school for PTA, new kids always asked dumb questions. "How'd your parents get so old?" "Is your dad sick or something?" "How come you don't have the same last name as them? Are you a foster kid?"

Then, I'd have to go over the whole thing. I wished I could just tell it once, and nobody would ever ask again. I used to think maybe I should write it out. The library had those copy things. I could make a million copies. Then, when people asked, I could hand them the whole story:

"I'm Mattie Jennings. I live with my grandmother and grandfather, Eleanor and Richard Weaver. My mom and dad had some bad trouble. They split up, and now they're married to other people. Period."

Gram and Gramps raised me from the time I was little. Gramps wasn't sick exactly. He was wounded in World War II. He had some heart trouble, too. He was a disabled veteran. He got a check from the government every month. It wasn't much. But, since Gramps didn't have a real job, he was always around to help Gram.

The two of them would get the house-work done real fast. As soon as I got home from school, we'd go to yard sales and flea markets.

Gramps liked to buy old junky stuff and fix it up like new. Then, we sold it. Gramps let me help him with the work. He showed me how to strip off the old paint and sand the wood smooth. (Most dads chase kids away when they're doing something interesting, but not Gramps.)

But the thing we did best was fishing—river fishing. We usually went to 'Gator Creek. Part of the name made sense. It did have alligators. But I never could understand why they called it a creek. It was a big river.

'Gator Creek wasn't too far from our house. But it was far enough that we liked to camp there overnight. That was better than driving home after a long day of fishing. Besides, Gramps liked to stay overnight so he could fish for catfish at night.

At first, we camped in a tent. Gram wasn't wild about camping. But she'd go along. She was afraid of the water. She'd never go near the boat. She said those Florida 'gators scared the liver out of her. The mosquitoes nearly ate her alive, too. And the woods were full of game in our part of Florida, near Tallahassee.

Sometimes, Gramps would fish all night. Gram hated that the most. She was alone with all the wild critters chirping and caterwauling all night.

One time, a skunk even stunk up the place. (Gram said she would never get that skunk stink out of her head.) We had to burn everything—clothes, sleeping bags, tent, the works.

Then, another time, a bunch of drunks came to the river. Gramps was there and drove them off. That's when Gram said, "That does it! No more camping for me!"

But nothing stopped Gramps. He got a camper truck. I'll never forget that! I was afraid Gram and Gramps might hang it up for good. I mean, it was open war.

Chapter 2

What Gramps did was trade in the Oldsmobile Cutlass for this Dodge camper truck. He never even asked Gram. He didn't even talk it over.

Gram didn't do a lot of social stuff like a lot of ladies her age. But she did belong to a little club. They played cards once a month. She really liked to drive. She got the car washed and slicked up. Then, she drove the ladies who didn't have cars. I think it was kind of a prestige thing with her. The Cutlass was a status symbol, I guess.

Gramps traded the Cutlass for the Dodge camper the morning of the bridge club. Gramps went out of the driveway with the Cutlass without even saying good-bye. Gram smelled a rat right off. She ran out the front door. "Where are you going with that car? I've got to get it washed today."

Gramps lied through his teeth. "Just going to get a *Sports Illustrated.*"

"Don't you dare come back late!"

Well, he didn't. He was gone only about 20 minutes. He had the deal cooked up days before.

Gramps had given out little hints. "You'll never guess the surprise I've got for you!" There were just a couple of things that had to be done to the camper before he got it. They put on a TV antenna, for one thing.

When Gramps came back, Gram was doing the dishes. The kitchen sink overlooked the driveway. She saw him pull in.

I heard her yell, "My God, Richard Weaver, what in the hell is that?" I had never heard Gram swear before in my life.

"Isn't she a beauty, Tootsie?"

"Don't you 'Tootsie' me, Richard Weaver! If you think I'm going to sit still for a thing like this, you're crazy. You take that thing right back where you got it. You get that Cutlass back here in ten minutes! If you don't, you'll just be a grease spot in the driveway."

"Tootsie, I can't do that. The Cutlass went in on the trade."

I'm not going to tell you what Gram said next. I couldn't believe the words that came out of her mouth.

In fact, she was letting Gramps have it with both barrels. Then, she looked around. She saw me standing there with my mouth open. I couldn't believe this was my dear old Gram.

Gram smashed the glass she was drying in the sink. She hid her face in her apron. She went sobbing up the stairs. She went to her room and locked her door. Gram had never acted like this as far back as I could remember.

Gramps came in the house. He looked at me. I mean, his face was serious. "Whoo, I guess I really did it this time."

He went up the stairs two at a time. He tried the bedroom door.

"Eleanor, honey, I wanted to surprise you. Wait till you see how nice it is inside. It has a real refrigerator and stove. The beds have real foam mattresses. There's even a little chemical toilet. We can go down to the Keys in it. Our motel will be right with us."

"You rotten old fool! You know that I'm taking the girls to bridge club tonight. Why in hell did you pick one that was orange?"

"I got a special deal on it, that's why. It's two years old. It's never been out of the showroom."

"Didn't you stop to wonder why? They had to wait two years to find a sucker like you."

"Listen, Eleanor, I'm sorry. I forgot about your club. I'll go over to Dave and explain everything. He'll let me have the Cutlass back to use tonight. I'll take it back tomorrow."

"You crazy fool. You don't think I'm going to the club after a thing like this? You're going to call the girls. Tell them I'm sick, because I am. I'm sick and tired of you. I'm tired of the way you never consider me. Not in anything you do! You're thoughtless and selfish. Get away from that door! I'm not coming out of here. And you're definitely not coming in."

Gramps quietly backed away. He came slowly down the stairs. I'm sure he thought that Gram would be tickled pink when she saw how nice the camper was.

Gramps went to the fridge and took out a beer. Then, he went to the camper. I followed him. I was all excited. I thought it was a great idea. I was dying to see what it was like inside. Except I was worried. Poor Gram! I followed Gramps out. "Can I come in?"

"Yes, Mattie. But don't expect much talk from me." He paused. "I guess surprises aren't such a good idea. I had no idea the Cutlass meant so much to your Gram."

I didn't look at him. I knew darn well he was lying. We both knew how much the Cutlass meant to Gram. That's why he hadn't talked it over with her. I didn't say anything. I just sat there.

"Well, say something, Mattie. Isn't this great?" He stood up and pushed up the ceiling vent hatch. "Isn't it great?" he asked again.

"You're lying, Gramps. We both know how much the Cutlass meant to Gram. You better call the ladies right now."

"I'll do better than that. I'll walk down to Dave's and get him to loan me the Cutlass. I'll drive the ladies to their club."

"But, without Gram, they'll have to play three-handed."

"I'll offer to sit in." And that's just what he did.

You wouldn't believe what Gram did then. As soon as Gramps was gone, she went out to the garage. She got a can of red paint. She turned on the light in the backyard. There she stood in her old robe and slippers. She painted in big red letters, "Richard Weaver is an old fool." On the other side of the truck, she painted a silly face. It was sticking out its tongue and wiggling its ears.

She didn't know that Gramps had talked Dave into calling off the deal. Gramps was going to take the camper back in the morning.

Gramps got home after playing cards with the ladies. He was in a really good mood. He knew he was going to make up with Gram. Their fights never did last long.

He came into the living room. There Gram sat, all dressed up. Her bags were packed. She had her speech rehearsed.

"Richard Weaver, you should have stayed a bachelor all your life. Today, I swore something awful in front of Mattie. I should have known I could expect things like this from you as long as I live. But I can't stand it anymore. I like to think I'm worthy of consideration. I'm leaving. I have some money in the bank from selling my potholders. You can sell the house and give me

my half. As soon as I have a job and I'm settled, I'll send for Mattie."

Her lips were quivering. Tears were running down her cheeks.

"Honey," Gramps said, "I'm taking the thing back in the morning. I explained to Dave, and he said it was no problem."

Gram's eyes got as big as saucers. I thought she'd faint. Then, she started to laugh. She laughed and laughed like she was hysterical.

I turned on the backyard light and took Gramps out. Gram followed us. She was laughing fit to split! Gramps took one look at the truck. He threw back his head and roared. He gave Gram a bear hug and kissed her like crazy. "Oh, Tootsie, you're the only girl for me!"

Gramps got out a bottle of wine and a candle. They sent me to bed. Those two crazy fools spent the night out in the camper.

Gram wanted to get the thing repainted. Gramps refused. "Where could I get such a classy decorator?" The camper became a conversation piece. All the kids at school were jealous. Gramps took a bunch of us fishing on the river. It was great.

There was only one bad thing. The camper was the only car we had. Gram felt funny about going to church in it. She wouldn't drive her friends to the club in it. But Dave came through. Dave loaned Gramps the Cutlass on club night. Gramps drove the "girls" to bridge club. Dave set the price of the Cutlass so high that no one would ever buy it.

One time, Gram and Gramps went to a flea market. They wanted to find some antiques. The stuff there turned out to be just "ticky-tacky," as Gramps called it. Little ceramic molded stuff. Fake flowers. Velvet pictures. That kind of stuff. But one lady had some new kinds of potholders made like hens and fish. Gram really liked them and stopped to look at them.

Gramps was in the parking lot, waiting for her. Just then, he saw this guy with these longhorns from a steer. They were fixed up to be mounted on the hood of your car. Gramps thought they were spectacular. This poor guy from Texas had sunk all his money into drilling an oil well on his land. But it turned out to be a dry hole. He took his last few bucks, went to a slaughterhouse, and bought up these horns cheap. Now, he was going around trying to sell them.

Folks in Texas liked the horns. But Florida people were more conservative. He hadn't sold one pair. So you know what? Gramps got a pair. The guy had a drill and bolts. He had them mounted on our hood by the time Gram got back.

You can imagine what that was like!

When Gramps bought the steer horns, it was Christmas time. The fishing was terrific on the river. But Gram didn't think we should be spending our time there. She wanted to have a tree and go to church, like a real Christmas.

"Richard, Mattie needs a more normal life. He needs friends his own age. We haul him off every weekend. It isn't right— especially at Christmas. It's important to have a real Christmas."

Well, by now you know Gramps. He went out that night. When he came back, we heard carols playing loud in the backyard. You should have seen the camper! Little twinkling Christmas lights were blinking on and off all over the longhorns. Dave had lent him the speaker and wired the lights for him.

Gramps took all the kids in my class caroling in the camper. We came back to our house for cocoa and popcorn. We called the truck Rudolph.

You guessed it. Then, we went to the river, Gramps and Gram and I—speakers and all. It was really cheery in the woods. We listened to carols and watched the lights twinkling.

"Richard Weaver, how do you do it? You make me do any darn fool thing—even against my better judgment."

"You think I'm persuasive? What about you? I swore I'd never set foot in church. You marched me down the aisle. And you get me there every Sunday that we're not on the river fishing."

"You go to church once in a blue moon. Fishing? You can't save your poor soul fishing! You swear a blue streak when you lose one!"

Gramps really did swear.

"When Christ was looking for good men, He went after fishermen, didn't He? They fished all night and didn't catch anything. Then, He told them to try the other side of the boat. I do stay out all night on the river. But that's what I'm waiting for. Someday, He'll tell me which side of the boat. We won't be able to haul the catch home, will we, Mattie?"

His voice changed. He was thinking. "Wouldn't it beat all if that's the kind of heaven He'd make! You'd fish all night and not be able to haul the catch home."

I can still hear him saying that in my head.

Chapter 3

The weekend I want to tell you about started when Gramps sold a maple dresser. We had found it at a yard sale. It was painted a wild blue color. Where the paint was chipped, Gramps could see that the wood was curly maple. It was the last thing left at the sale. So the lady paid us to haul it away.

Gramps let me help him fix up the dresser. After we got through with it, it was a real beauty!

It was a Friday in April when Gramps sold the dresser for $100. That was some day! To celebrate, we went shopping after school. Gramps got me the catcher's mitt I had always wanted. He got Gram a new Sunday dress she really liked. (To me, it looked just like all her other dresses—pink flowers.) Gram and I insisted that Gramps get himself a new fly rod he had his eye on—for river fishing.

After supper, we celebrated some more with root beer floats. (We made our own root beer, and was it good!) Then, I had a great idea.

"When I grow up, I'm going to have a store to sell Gramps's antiques. I'll take care of you, instead of you taking care of me."

Gramps squeezed Gram's hand. They looked at each other and then at me. Gram jumped up from the table and started doing dishes. Gramps said, "Come on, Mattie. Let's get some fresh air."

It was late. I should have been in bed. But it had been one of those great days. So much good stuff had happened. We just couldn't let it go.

We went out into the night. I can still hear the screen door bang behind us as we went. I can still smell the sweet air.

That night the breeze smelled like flowers and grass. It went through my hair and down my neck inside my shirt. It sent a shiver right straight through me. Gramps shivered, too.

"I can't wait to try out that fly rod tomorrow," he said. "We can set out our trotline for catfish, too. From the sunset, I'd say the weather looks perfect. Let's talk Gram into it."

I wish I could be walking down that street with Gramps again, the way we were that Friday night. I'd say, "Gramps, I don't want to go fishing tomorrow. Let's play ball instead."

We did play catch for a while that night. But Gramps kept grabbing his shoulder. Finally, he said that we'd better stop. "Rheumatism," he called it.

When we went back in the house, Gram put up a mild fight about camping that weekend. She always did.

"I have a new dress to wear to church Sunday. Mattie has a new mitt to play with the kids. You want us to give up what we want, for what you want. Isn't that a little bit selfish?"

Gramps shrugged his shoulders. He sort of slumped down in the kitchen chair.

I know why he hated church. When he put on a suit and tie and all, he looked like he was dressed up for Halloween. It was like his clothes didn't really belong to him. His coat hiked up at the collar. He slicked his hair down. But there was still a bunch at the back that stood straight up. (I've got one, too. It's called a cowlick.) His shirt and tie looked like they were about to choke him. His shoes, all shiny and new, showed the outline of his little toes. He walked like his feet were killing him.

As we rode to church, Gram would always say, "Now, try to be pleasant today, Richard."

"How can I, when I'm feeling so darned uncomfortable! I'll bet Jesus couldn't smile when his feet hurt."

"Richard, don't talk like that! I want to go out for Sunday dinner, too. I have the money."

"Well, I want to get home. I want to get out of this monkey suit. It's not good for anything but marrying and burying."

Usually, there would be a long pause. Gram would fake a few sniffles. Then, Gramps would say in his most winning way, "I'd rather put my feet under your table than eat steak in any rest-stew-rant."

Gramps always said rest-stew-rant. Gram always corrected him. He'd give her hand a squeeze, and she'd say, "Oh, all right. Hitch up the boat while I make sandwiches."

"Yahooee!" Gramps would step on the gas, and we'd be home in a minute. We'd spend Sunday fishing on the river. Gram would read the Sunday paper or sew in the beach chair on the bank.

But there was one thing about church Gramps did love. That was singing. Gramps had a favorite hymn. They never played it in church, but he taught it to me, anyway. It went like this:

> Father, Father, through the night
> Guard me till the day is light.
> Wrap me in Thy boundless love
> From below and from above.
> You have made me wondrously.
> Someday, I'll know the mystery.
> God as Father, Earth as Mother,
> Every living thing my brother.
> When I sail that final sea,
> Your loving arms will welcome me.

"That final sea" meant death. I knew that. It gave me the shivers to hear him sing that hymn. His head was thrown back. His great mouth let out those strange and terrifying words.

I saw a dead bird once. I slept with the light on for a week. Even our dead fish bothered me. Gramps knew what I was thinking. "God provides fish for our table. That's why Gram says grace."

"I don't think there is a God," I told him. "How could He make people just so they can die?"

"How could He make folks so they wouldn't die? What if everyone who ever lived were still alive? There wouldn't be room to stand up." He stopped talking for a little while. "And when you're worn out, it's no fun hanging around."

"It stinks," I said. He didn't answer.

What would happen to me if anything happened to Gram and Gramps? I thought I'd just about die, and I said so.

"No, you wouldn't," Gramps said. "If anything happened to me, you'd take care of your Gram. Then, you'd take very good care of yourself. When you'd go fishing and catch a big one, I'd be right there. In spirit, I'd say, 'Go get 'em, Mattie!'"

He'd tousle my hair and pull my head down. I'd try to wiggle out. He'd put a head lock on me. It was his way of hugging me. It felt good and safe and close.

"That'll be a mighty long time from now," Gramps said. "You and Gram will be sick of me before I go."

Chapter 4

Like I said, when Gramps and I got back from walking and playing ball that Friday night, Gram put up a little fuss about going fishing that weekend.

She was putting away the root beer glasses when we came in. The screen door gave its usual *wham*. Gramps gave Gram a smooch.

"You two have been hatching up something. Richard, your face has *fishing* written all over it."

"And camping," I added.

She threw her apron down in mock disgust. "I knew it! I knew it! Leave you two together five minutes, and I'm licked."

"And outnumbered!" Gramps added. Gramps looked sheepish, but his eyes twinkled. "The camping gear is already packed. It's in the bottom of the boat."

"That's why you lashed the canvas down. I should have known," Gram said.

"Yes, you should have. And you should have bought hot dogs. Corn meal to fry the fish in. And pancake mix. And lemons for lemonade and—"

"Stop right there!" Gram said. "I already did. Look in the pantry. There are boxes of groceries ready to go. Even the suitcases are packed."

Gramps thumped the table with his fist. Some people do this in anger. Gramps did it when he was delighted. When words failed him, he thumped.

"You mean you don't care if you miss church?" he asked. "You won't miss wearing your new dress?"

"No, I don't care. Mildred Tanner said she got a new dress. It sounds like the same one."

Gramps roared his famous roar. "Tootsie, I'll make a woods lady out of you yet!"

"No, you won't," Gram said. "But I've decided that if you can't lick 'em, join 'em. I'm taking a baseball bat for the critters. And I've got a juicy love story. I'll read it by the Coleman lantern. You can fish till the sun comes up. I won't care."

Was she bluffing?

"Mattie, your Gram has real class. The smartest thing I ever did was to marry her."

"You'll never get me in a boat on that river, though," Gram said. "Those alligators swimming around all night scare the liver out of me. Besides, this is a bargain. You're going to take me to the Bon Appetit restaurant. Our thirty-first anniversary is June fifteenth. So there!"

"Don't count on it!"

"Richard Weaver, you good-for-nothing bloodworm! You'd better promise. Otherwise, you'll go fishing over my dead body!" A strange shiver went through me. I hated to hear talk about dead bodies, even in fun.

"Let's cross that bridge when we come to it."

"I'm serious, Richard. I won't budge till you say yes."

"We'll see," he answered. He went out the door with the groceries.

"You have to promise!" Gram hollered after him.

"All right. The Good Lord willing, we'll go to the Bon Appetit. But if it's not on the Lord's agenda, it's out." He was off with another box to the camper.

Gram gave him a look that said, "You'd better not go back on your word to me, Richard Weaver."

Then, Gramps went stomping upstairs. Gram banged the silverware drawer shut. She noisily put the dinner pots and pans away.

"Are you coming upstairs, Gram?" I asked. I never liked it when Gram and Gramps didn't go to bed at the same time.

"No, I'm going to simmer down. I want to read the paper."

She was upset, I could tell. I went to my room and got ready for bed. Still, Gram didn't come up.

About 20 minutes went by. Gramps stomped to the head of the stairs. "Eleanor, get up here! I can't sleep if you're still up!" Gramps was annoyed.

"Do we go to the Bon Appetit?"

"I told you yes once!"

I heard the light switch off. "OK." Gram came up.

Chapter 5

Gramps and I both had fishing on our minds all night. We talked about it in the morning.

I dreamed he let me cast with his new fly rod. The line landed right in a weed bed. Then, I pulled it out. There was a 12-pound carp on the line. I was just about to land him when a 'gator snapped him up.

I was dragged into the water. I was pulled by that crazy 'gator faster than spit. I wouldn't let go of the rod. I didn't want to lose it.

Finally, I got up on my feet. I was on the water, skiing. The riverbank was lined with people cheering. Then, the line broke.

I woke up. I tried to go back to sleep. Did I lose the rod? I couldn't get back into my dream. I just lay there, thinking about the river. Where would we set up camp?

Pretty soon, I heard someone moving around. Gramps's slippers went shuffling past my door. He was on his way to the kitchen. I smelled coffee. It was just starting to get light out. I had my jeans and Boy Scout sweatshirt on the chair. I put them on.

I went to the kitchen. Gramps had the Sunoco map stretched out on the table. He was looking at 'Gator Creek.

"Mattie, I think I've found the perfect spot. Look at the map. See where the river makes an elbow turn? See that piece of land in the middle where the river swings around like the letter C?"

I nodded.

"That piece of land is cleared. It's up high enough for a nice, dry camp. The river is deep there. We can tie up to a bald cypress tree that's growing out of the bank. That's the spot, all right."

He sipped his coffee and went on. "Eleanor will feel safe there. She'll have water on two sides. The truck will protect the other side. I want to get there before someone else does. I sure hope that woman doesn't sleep until noon!" He sounded impatient.

Neither of us heard Gram come into the kitchen.

"That woman," Gram surprised us, "is the only one washed and dressed. Her teeth are brushed, too."

I ran my tongue over my teeth. I hadn't brushed. I hadn't washed. How could she tell without seeing my face?

Darned if she wasn't ready to go. It was only five o'clock. The birds were just starting to twitter.

Gramps liked to complain about Gram. It was his way of making conversation. Gram knew this. Still, sometimes it made her mad. Or was she hurt?

"Don't make me out to be your big, old wife," she would say. "If you do, I'll let you have it." She never would, of course. We all knew that.

There were things we knew, but never talked about. Even though Gram insisted we'd go to the Bon Appetit for their anniversary, we all knew better. We'd have steaks at home instead. Gramps would bring home a bottle of wine. They'd even give me some, just to make it a real celebration. Then, we'd sing around the piano. Finally, we'd sing Gramps's favorite hymn, "Father, Father, through the night, guard me till the morning light."

Gram would try to fake it on the piano. We didn't have that hymn in a book. In fact, no one had ever heard of it but Gramps. Every time we'd get together with people, Gramps would ask if anybody knew this hymn. Nobody ever did. In fact, he couldn't remember what church he learned it in. That was back in Arkansas, when he was a boy.

Gram would say, "Why do you care about a thing like that?"

Gramps would say, "I don't know. It's like I've lost something important. I want to find a copy of that hymn before I die. It's kind of my song."

"That's mighty odd for a man who hates church so much," Gram would say.

"It's not church I hate. It's getting dressed up. Those disciples went around in any old rags that would cover their bones. How did this getting dressed up ever get started?"

"It's just respectful."

"Respectful, hell! It's pure torment. A necktie stops the blood to my head. That's why I fall asleep in church."

I hated all the arguments about going to church. The way I talk about Gramps's cussing, you probably think he was a bad man. But for all his talk, he had a kind heart.

Three old ladies lived alone on our street. He carried out their trash and mowed their grass. If they thought they heard a burglar, they never called the police. They called Gramps. (Gram swore that one of the ladies was sweet on Gramps. She was *always* hearing burglars.)

Gramps really sounded like a heathen, except when he was singing his song. At least, this week there was no argument about church. We were going to the river—to fish.

'Gator Creek is no good for swimming. That's not just because of the 'gators. It has water moccasins, too—and copperheads. We've got lots of snakes in Florida, and all kinds of bugs, too.

So, since we always went river fishing, I never learned how to swim. Gramps was always going to take us down to Big Pine Key. I could learn to swim in the ocean easy. Salt water holds you up.

I was going to learn to swim at the YMCA. But the classes always came when we were getting in a lot of good fishing. I just sort of never did.

Gramps bought me a life jacket. It was so uncomfortable! When we'd get to where we wanted to fish, he'd let me take it off. I'd say, "Gramps, this thing is so hot and uncomfortable. Can't I take it off until we're ready to go back?"

"Oh, all right. But no walking around in the boat, mind you."

Gramps made our anchor out of an old bucket filled with cement. He tied it with a rope to the ring on the front of the boat.

When we found a good spot, he'd throw out the bucket. We'd drift downstream as far as the rope would let us. When we were ready to go back, he'd pull it back up. It wasn't easy, against the current.

Well, back to what happened that day. Quick as you could say "spit," we had breakfast. We did the dishes and hitched up the boat trailer.

It wasn't even six o'clock yet. We were going down the back roads toward the elbow of 'Gator Creek.

Our camper truck was the kind that went over the cab. But we never rode back there. I always rode up front between Gram and Gramps. Gram knew how to read road maps. And she was teaching me. Of course, we knew the river so well, we almost didn't need a map. But we used it, anyway. The back roads in Florida are tricky. You can get lost real easy. Everything grows so fast. Things never look the same way twice.

At the elbow, there was always lots of fast water going by in the spring. It sort of dug out the dirt. It made a steep curved side in the bank. It was too steep for 'gators to crawl up. (They're mean, but they're clumsy.) We never camped where the ground sloped down gently to the water. That was 'gator territory.

Besides water moccasins and 'gators, there were wild pigs and deer. In fact, there were all kinds of critters. Possum and turtles. (Possum pie and turtle soup, now there's a meal for you!)

You're allowed to set out 25 hooks on trotlines. We usually split them up three hooks to a line and spread them out. Then, we'd go putt-putting back to camp. Gram usually had something good cooking, even on the camp stove. She had rigged up an oven on that thing. She could even bake sweet potato pie and hot biscuits.

Well, getting back to that day. Camp was set up. Gram was sitting in a deck chair. She had her needlework in her lap. We were getting our gear together for our first fishing run.

Our campsite was in a grove of young trees. They had slender trunks. A lot of the branches and growth were at the very top. The morning sunlight came through in long streaks. The packed-down, damp earth shone. The grass was bright green. The trees were sort of whispering in the breeze of early morning.

In the afternoon, everything would be stone quiet. The only sound would be the water gurgling a little as it went around the bend. Of course, in the afternoon, the bugs would start buzzing. I guess, come to think of it, the woods and the river are never all the way quiet. But you could tell what time it was, even if you were blind. The sounds and the temperature told you.

A lot of birds were chirping. An old kingfisher was the only bird you could see. He sat on a branch over the water. Then, he'd fly and dive down. He'd come up with a little silver fish in his beak. He'd go back to his branch and give one gulp. The fish was gone. Then, he'd dive again.

"The river's so muddy, Gramps. How does the kingfisher know where the fish are?"

"He sees the quick flash of that silver body moving under the surface. The fish come up for water bugs. The bird comes down for the fish. Anybody who thinks Mother Nature is all love and kisses hasn't looked around much."

We rolled the boat trailer close to the edge. Then, we slid the boat off and down the steep bank. We tied it to the old cypress. What surprised me was that Gramps left the motor in the boat while we slid it down the bank. It didn't get damaged or anything. But that Johnson motor was his baby. Usually, he took it off the boat while he put the boat in the water. Then, he carried the motor down to the water himself.

I had to put on my clumsy, old orange life jacket. I climbed down the roots. They were exposed on the side of the riverbank. They were like steps. Gramps handed down his new rod, my pole, and the bait bucket. His tackle box was already in the boat. So were the big, oversized safety cushions Gramps had custom made. ("Those things cost more than my living room couch!" Gram used to say. Gramps would just give her a look like, "That's a stupid remark.") Then, Gramps climbed down into the boat himself.

Gram had her chair in a two-foot square patch of sunshine. She was threading her needle.

Gramps said, "Eleanor, I'm going to untie the rope at the front of the boat instead of the rope around the tree. That'll be easier when we come back. I won't have to throw that thing up there." His shoulder must have been aching.

"Couldn't you just let Mattie climb up with it? Don't you need a rope on the front of the boat?"

"Of course. I've got another one I'm going to put on. When we come back, I'll just tie them together. This rheumatism is teaching me things I should have thought of before!"

With that, he started the motor. He stood upright in the boat. He started singing. He sang his second-favorite song to Gram as we went down the river. "Toot-Toot-Tootsie, good-bye. Toot-Toot-Tootsie, don't cry. I'll never fail, travel by rail, if you don't get a letter, then you know I'm in jail."

Gram yelled after us, "Sit down in the boat, you old fool!" As soon as we were out of sight, Gramps sat down. Why was everything he was doing scaring the liver out of me?

Chapter 6

"Come on, Mattie. I want you to get used to steering this thing. Keep your weight in the middle of the boat and get back here. I'll sit on the middle seat, so you'll have the whole show to yourself."

"Why can't I sit beside you?"

"With us both in the back, the front would go up. The boat isn't as stable that way."

He was worrying me. I told him so. "Why did you stand up in the boat back there? You were clowning around. It scares me when you do that."

"Mattie, you sound more like your grandmother every day." His voice changed. "You're right, as usual. I guess I'm just so glad to be alive. I want to make every minute spectacular."

I wanted to hug him.

We were coming to his favorite fly casting spot. He had me cut the engine. We drifted into just the right spot. He pitched out the anchor. His face twisted up like that really hurt.

Then, he let me take off my life jacket. He got out the bloodworms for me. The flies were for him.

My pole was bamboo, with a weight and bobber. He tied on a new fish hook with a special barrel knot for tying nylon monofilament line. (I can do it myself now.)

I always kind of loved and hated threading the bloodworm onto the hook. It twisted and turned and tickled my hand. I couldn't cut one in half with my fingernail like Gramps. He tried to teach me. But he knew I didn't like to do it. Besides, I bite my nails.

"The trick, son, is to thread the bloodworm on your hook, not on your finger."

It had to be the most marvelous day that ever was. Even sounds were beautiful. I loved the little plop and gurgle as the sinker went into the water.

"Good throw, Mattie," Gramps whispered. There it was, that little electric thrill. His words spoke right to my heart.

Zing went his new fly line. He was slowly reeling it in, back and forth. I sat and waited. I was first. That red bobber went way down. I gave the pole a hard jerk. Then, I had to put the pole down. I hauled in the line hand over hand. Then, I pulled him out. Five inches of feisty sunfish. I unhooked him and tossed him back. "See you next year," I told him.

Gramps got a nice river bass. And, then, it was lunch time.

Gramps kind of groaned as he pulled up the anchor. He hauled it into the boat. He made me put on my life jacket. We started the engine and headed back to camp. Putt, putt, putt.

"Let's just leave our stuff in the boat this time. We're going out after lunch. What's the harm?" Gramps said.

This was strange. Gramps always took everything out of the boat. Even if we were just going back to check on Gram, he did. We often came back to keep her company for a while. Leaving the gear in the boat sounded like a good idea, just different. I hated hauling all that junk up.

Gram had rigged a rope to the tree. So we had something to hang onto. I came up the bank on the root steps. I was up in two shakes.

Gram said, "Where's Gramps?" He heard her and hollered from the boat. "I drowned!" He was straightening out his lure box, I think. Gramps was such a fussbudget about his fishing tackle. Everything else could go hang.

Gram started setting the table for lunch. Gramps came up at last. But he forgot to bring his river bass up. "No lunch for me yet," he said. "I'm going to get a little shut-eye. I was practicing casting all night. And we were up at the crack of dawn."

"We certainly were," Gram said. "Well, I'll bet you're ready for lunch, aren't you, Mattie?"

Gram was right. I was starving.

Gram had sandwiches all ready. We sat down together. Egg salad and lettuce, with a little dill pickle—my favorite.

"How did it go?" she asked.

"Gramps caught a nice river bass. It's still on the stringer. It's over the side of the boat."

"You'd better bring it up before something gets it." She was right. When I brought it up, the tail was already gone.

"Imagine that," I said. Anything hanging around in that water wouldn't last long.

I asked Gramps about it when he got up. "What do you suppose got it?"

"Who knows?" was all he said. "It's the law of nature."

We cleaned what was left of the fish.

"Suppose it's OK to eat?" I asked.

"Why not?" Gramps never worried unnecessarily.

"It will make a delicious dinner," Gram said.

I caught her taking careful peeks at Gramps out of the corner of her eye. She didn't want him to notice. She was looking at him very carefully.

"I knew my great fisherman would come through." She gave Gramps a hug and smoothed his hair. He hated that.

"Do you suppose she's sweet on me? Or do you suppose she's just taking out insurance on that trip to the Bon Appetit?"

"Are we going back fishing now?" I asked. Gramps seemed to be just sitting around. I wanted to have a fish of my own for dinner. Gramps's fish would feed two, but not three. Besides, I wanted to land a keeper.

"It's a warm afternoon," Gramps said. "Nothing will be biting now. If you want to fish, throw your line off the bank. Or go sit in the boat. But put on your life jacket. I'm going to get some more sleep. We go for catfish tonight."

I really wanted Gramps to take the boat out. I was about to go into my begging routine. But one look from him told me not to.

I did go down in the boat for a while. I put on my life jacket. Nothing was biting. I felt hot and sticky. A pesky fly kept flying around me. It was one of those deerflies. He bit me real bad, so I got out of there. This fishing trip was becoming very boring.

I came up on the bank. Gramps decided to go out in the boat. He was going to set out catfish lines all down the bank. He had rigged up 25 hooks on trotlines, mind you. Gramps knew lots of poor people. He tried to take them as much fish as he could. We weren't rich. But there were lots of people poorer than us. When he did something like that, Gram would say, "You're a good old coot, Richard Weaver!"

And he'd say, "Heck, no! I'm the meanest man around!"

Gramps went alone to set out his lines. It was too hot for me. I got out my comics. I found a cool spot on the blanket. Pretty soon, it was supper time.

Gram must have prayed over that fish, because there was plenty for dinner. (I think she used to bring some from the meat market.) Man, did I eat! Fried fish, potato salad, greens, and tomatoes. Then, some of Gram's great chocolate cake.

After we cleaned up the dinner mess, Gramps said, "What do you say we take another snooze? We can go out about nine o'clock and check the lines. We can stay out all night if we have to. If you get tired, you can sleep on the cushion in the bottom of the boat."

But Gramps knew that I never got tired of fishing. Gram shook her head. "You're two of a kind. More's the pity." That would sound like a slam unless you heard her say it. She kind of shrugged her shoulders. Then, she sort of tilted her head to one side. The laughing-scolding in her voice let you know not to take her seriously. She'd be shocked if you did.

So we bunked down for a snooze. Gramps even set the alarm on his watch.

Gram said, "If I lie down now, I'll be awake all night waiting for you two to come home. That would be dumb. I'm going to watch the twilight. Then, I'll read my book by the Coleman lantern. Don't set the alarm. I'll wake you."

"No, you won't," Gramps said. "You'll let us sleep all night. You think I look tired or something. That'll be your excuse. You won't wake us because you hate being here alone at night."

I guess Gramps was right about all those things. Maybe if he'd left things to Gram, life would be different.

Chapter 7

Anyway, the alarm went off at nine. I was up like a shot. I never really fell asleep. I just kept daydreaming. I guess you'd call it night dreaming—about fishing.

There wasn't a tinge of daylight left. When it gets dark in Florida, it happens in a hurry. It was pitch black in our camp. The beam of Gramps's big flashlight shone up on the whitish underside of the leaves overhead. It shone ahead to the light bark of the young trees. Gram flipped on the lights on the longhorns to give us a cheery good-bye. They looked so cute, blinking out there in the woods.

Gram held the flashlight for us so we could find the roots to climb down. Our shadows looked huge. They stretched clear across the water to the woods on the other side. Why they call this river 'Gator *Creek,* I'll never know. It's enormous. It seems even bigger at night.

We were in the boat and untied in a minute. We began drifting. We were out from the bank and in the channel. Gramps got the motor started. "Mattie, get that life jacket on this minute!" he said.

What was Gramps afraid of? Was he mad at me, or what?

Now that we were out on the river, you could look straight up at the stars twinkling overhead. It was very different from the black of the woods. The sky looked dark, dark blue. It was sprinkled with diamonds. The moon looked like a giant orange coming up over the river. It made an orange ribbon on the black water in front of us.

"Now, son, ease down to this end of the boat. With this moonlight, I'm going to give you your first lesson in night piloting."

My heart jumped into my mouth. I wasn't ready for this.

"You can do it, son. You just ride that moonbeam." This was unreal. I was really doing it! I was running the boat on the river in the moonlight.

Gramps had the flashlight. He was searching the bank for the stakes he drove in the soft mud to hold the trotlines.

"What if all the hooks have fish on them?" I asked. "We'll swamp the boat!"

"Those are the problems of prosperity, Mattie. You just have to cope with good fortune!"

I could see we were going past trotlines every couple of yards. Gramps was counting them. When we got to the end of the lines, we'd start working our way back. We would check to see if we had any catfish. If there were no fish, we'd wait a couple of hours. With the moon so bright, the fish would really be feeding.

We were at the end of the stakes.

"OK, Mattie. Cut the motor while I throw out the anchor." I heard him pick up the anchor. I already had my life jacket off. I was baiting my hook. I was going to fish while Gramps checked the line. That was a one-man job. I was going to catch me a fish—a really big fish.

I heard Gramps struggling and groaning with the anchor. Suddenly, he screamed with pain, "Oh! Oh, my God!" I could feel the boat tipping. Then, Gramps fell over the side with the anchor in his arms. The whole boat capsized.

I was in the water. I got a mouthful. I sputtered and gurgled. I kept working my hands and feet to stay afloat. Gramps called my name once. Then, he and the boat were gone.

I was coughing and choking and gasping for air. I couldn't say a word. It was like something awful had me by the throat.

Then, something hit me on the back of the neck. It was one of those oversized cushions from the boat. Gramps had always told me, "If the boat ever turns over, grab one of those cushions. Don't let go till help comes."

I grabbed onto the cushion. Everything was so quiet. I couldn't believe it. Gramps must have made it to shore and gone for help.

I found my voice. I called out, again and again. "Gramps! Gramps! Where are you? Gramps, I'm here! I'm OK!"

How could he go off like this? How could he leave me with the 'gators and whatever got the river bass?

Something touched my toe. "Oh, God! Oh, God!" I kicked my feet violently. I had to get on top of the cushion. I tried to scoot myself up onto it. The force shoved it under water. I had visions of it floating away from me.

This time, I pushed with a big flop—like a fish does. I got straight across it. Then, I carefully got my right knee over the edge.

Something nibbled at my other foot. I kicked out at it. I almost forced myself off the cushion. It went down under me. But, then, I was able to get my knee up under my chest. I got my whole self up on the cushion.

Carefully, I turned myself around and sat down on the cushion. My feet were in the water. Something big touched my foot again. I pulled both feet out of the water violently. I almost fell off backwards. But, now, I was able to cross my legs under me, Indian fashion.

I listened for the sound of someone going through the underbrush. I called again and again, "Gramps! Gramps!" There was only the sound of a loon to answer me. Then, I heard something. Something big was sliding into the water.

'Gators! It had to be 'gators! It couldn't be Gramps. Then, I heard something again. It sounded like a big log rolling into the water.

In the moonlight, things broke the orange ribbon on the water. They looked like rough logs. Around and around me they went. They were 'gators—two 'gators, swimming around me.

I made growling sounds. I splashed and slapped the water. I slapped with the flat of my palms. It made a loud sound. Sound is louder under water. I knew that. I kept slapping the water again and again. It must have been hours that those 'gators circled me.

The moon had moved up in the sky. It was overhead. I strained my eyes. I watched the water for any sign of those circling logs. I could see nothing but the reflection of a million stars on the black water.

I must be drifting with the current, I thought. Where would it take me?

If Gramps had gone for help, would he even know where to look for me? The boat was gone for sure.

About 20 miles from where we were fishing, the river narrowed. All that water went roaring through the rocky shoals. I had heard about the shoals. But I had never seen them. In the spring, the water is high. It crashes through those big boulders,

smashing everything into bits. And it was spring now.

What if I drifted that far? Could I paddle myself to the bank with my hands? Would there be 'gators on the bank when I got there?

The loon kept making its awful calls. Yet, at least, it was a sound.

I decided to sing to myself. I decided to sing all the songs I knew. I started with Christmas carols. Then, I sang our Scout songs. I said the Boy Scout oath. I said the code of the pack. I said my multiplication tables. I subtracted numbers in my head.

I said all my Bible verses. I said the names of all the kids in my class. I said the names of the books of the Bible. I said the names of all our neighbors. I said the names of the kinds of cars they drove. I said the names of their dogs and cats.

Gramps used to say, "When you're scared, Mattie, think of something funny. It clears your head." So, I thought of all the TV comedies I liked best. It really did help.

I couldn't see the moon anymore. It was behind me now. I was feeling drowsy. The 'gators were gone. To keep myself awake, I tried to imagine they were there. But my head would start to drop to my chest. I would feel it and jerk myself awake.

I splashed water on my hands and face. That worked. It woke me up.

Chapter 8

The sky was turning pink. Birds were beginning to chirp. I saw a mother deer and her fawn standing in the water drinking. They looked at me curiously. They ran into the woods.

It was really getting to be morning now. The sky was beautiful colors. I began to sing again, just to hear my own voice. I couldn't believe I was still alive. It was Gramps's hymn I sang:

> Father, Father, through the night
> Guard me till the day is light.
> Wrap me in Thy boundless love
> From below and from above.
> You have made me wondrously.
> Someday, I'll know the mystery.
> God as Father, Earth as Mother,
> Every living thing my brother.
> When I sail that final sea,
> Your loving arms will welcome me.

Then, the tears started running down my face. Surely, Gramps would be coming soon. Why was he taking so long? It wasn't like him to be so slow.

The sun was coming over the trees now, I knew. From the east, it shone on the water. I could feel its warm rays on my back and head. That was the first time I realized I was covered with goose bumps. I'd been shivering all night.

The sun felt great! The hymn says, "God as Father, Earth as Mother." But what about the sun? It was pouring life into me. It was like breakfast. And that thought reminded me that I was starving.

Gramps should have come by now. Where was he? I was starting to be angry at him. He left me all night without coming to get me!

Maybe some other fishermen were around. I was drifting past low, muddy banks. Sure enough, there was an "old log" in the water. It yawned without opening its eyes and went back to sleep. At first, I was glad to be able to see things. But, at night, it was as hard for the 'gators to see me, as it was for me to see them.

Now, I'd be a real target. I could see them coming. But where could I hide? I'd be just like the river bass on the stringer. I'd be waiting for something to snap me up—piece by piece.

The sun was getting really hot now. I was breaking out in sweat from fear. Where was Gramps? Could he be just sitting around having a cup of coffee? It was full daylight now.

He wouldn't do that. Maybe he got turned around. Maybe he got lost in the woods in the dark. That would be easy to do. You couldn't get directions from the stars in the woods. The trees were too thick overhead. So maybe he had just been wandering around in the woods all night! With the sun up, he'd be able to find the road and get help.

I splashed fresh water on my face. I even cupped my hands and drank some. It tasted fishy. But Gramps had always told me, "Drinking running water—miles from nowhere—is safer than getting dehydrated." All I could get was maybe typhoid or malaria. I really hoped I lived long enough to get sick!

In the distance, I heard a rumbling. It could have been thunder. But there were no clouds. The sun was bright. It must be the rocky shoals, I thought. I had been drifting all night. I must be coming to the shoals.

In the night, I had strained my eyes to see in the dark. Now, I strained my ears to hear. I tried to sift out the sounds. There were birds. There was the buzzing of insects. There were all the sounds that come alive with the sun.

I happened to look at my arms. I had a million mosquito bites! Now that I saw them, they started to itch. Just because I knew they were there, I guess. I scratched and scratched till the blood ran.

Anyway, it was good to feel the bites. "Dead people don't itch," I told myself.

I couldn't believe Gramps would leave me alone like this. It was getting hotter and hotter. I was sweaty and sticky. The thunder was louder. I was sure it was the rocky shoals.

One bank was less steep than the other. I tried to use my hands as paddles to get there. But the current was swifter now.

In places, there were rocks. Water eddied around them. My cushion started turning and going sideways. It moved much faster now. The roar was very loud. In fact, I could see where the smooth edge of the shining water ended. The current spilled into the jagged rocks of the shoals.

Nothing could save me now. I was terrified. I'll die brave, like an Indian, I thought. I started to sing Gramps's hymn again.

I clung to the cushion. It turned crazily around and around. It swooshed sideways between the rocks.

Something struck me on the chest and knocked me off the cushion. It was a cable! Someone had stretched a cable clear across the river. It was just 10 feet from terrible rocks. "Thank God! Thank God!" I yelled. I clung to the cable. I watched the cushion disappear into the rocks.

The water dragged my legs ahead of me. I knew I had to conserve my strength. I stretched out, full length. I gripped the cable with my hands. It felt good to straighten my legs. They were cramped from sitting cross-legged all night.

There were no 'gators here. Maybe I could even slide my hands one at a time

toward the shore. Maybe I could drag myself away from the swiftest current.

The cable was rusty. I could see blood running down my arms. My hands were raw from the cable. Some loose wires had slashed me.

I couldn't sing anymore. I couldn't think anymore. I just started to cry. I cried and cried and cried.

Something in me was saying, "Give up. Let go. Just let it happen."

The roar of the thundering water was a hypnotic sound. It was like a giant electric fan. The roar was so loud that I didn't hear the other sound—a power boat.

"There he is! My God, he's still alive!"

Chapter 9

The rest of that day is a giant blur. I vaguely remember being wrapped in someone's overcoat. Gram kissed my face and smoothed my hair. She sobbed huge sobs that shook her like an earthquake. But no Gramps.

"Where's Gramps?" I finally found the courage to ask Gram.

"We don't know yet, dear. We don't know."

Maybe he was wandering around in the woods. Maybe he was just lost.

The men with Gram started asking me questions. "Do you remember anything about the place where you were fishing? Anything at all?"

I told them what I knew. "It was so dark, you know. I couldn't see a thing. We were going for catfish. We had trotlines pegged

to the bank. We were at the last peg. Did
you see the stakes in the bank?"

That was all they needed. The men were
off again.

The sheriff took Gram and me home. She
didn't want to go. But he insisted. I think
he knew what they were going to find. He
didn't want her there.

Gram lay down on the bed with me. She patted me like I was a little baby. She put her warm arms around me. I felt like someone had pulled the plug in my head. My brains had all drained out. I was a glob of Jell-O.

"You need something in your stomach," Gram said. "I'll fix some soft-boiled eggs and toast. How about a cup of tea with lots of cream and sugar?"

Gram went to the kitchen. I drifted off to sleep. Suddenly, I heard the sound of men's boots on the front porch. The screen door slammed. The men came into the living room. From the sound of the boots, there must have been five or six men. Then, it got very quiet. One man's voice was very low.

I jumped out of bed. I ran to the top of the stairs to listen.

"We found Richard and the boat in twenty-five feet of water. We took him to Benson's Funeral Home. Is that all right?"

There wasn't any other funeral home nearby.

The man went on, "They're getting the boat and motor up now."

Gram's voice was loud and clear. "Don't bring that thing here. Sell it cheap. Get rid of it."

"You do want us to drive the camper back, don't you?"

Gram sighed a heavy sigh. "I guess so." She was sobbing now. She managed to say, "Thank you."

"Something is burning in the kitchen," one of the men said.

I could smell it, too. The eggs had boiled dry and were burning. I ran downstairs and turned off the stove.

I knew Gram needed me now. I wanted her to know that I would do what Gramps would want me to do.

She was sitting in the rocking chair. I threw my arms around her. She pulled me onto her lap, big as I was. We cried in each other's necks.

Chapter 10

Somehow, we did all the things you're supposed to do.

Strange ladies came and brought piles of food. Relatives we hadn't seen in ages showed up. Newspaper guys wanted pictures of me. Gram just let them have an old picture of me in my Boy Scout shirt.

People wanted to stay with us overnight. Gram kicked them all out.

The next morning, Gram had to take Gramps's Sunday suit and stuff to Benson's. They came and picked her up in a big black car.

That night, they had calling hours at the funeral home. Gram wanted me to stay with some friends because I was so shook up. I wanted to be there with her.

She needed me.

I got all dressed up in my best clothes. Gram wore her new pink dress.

She said, "I'll bet Mabel Hunt will have a few things to say about my wearing pink. But Richard hated black—or even navy blue."

That was true. One time, Gram bought a black dress. She came home and put it on.

"What do you think, Richard?" she asked.

"Take that thing off! Don't you ever buy another black dress as long as I'm alive. And don't you dare wear a black dress to my funeral. I'll rise up out of my coffin and strip you bare as a baby's butt!"

Gram laughed till she almost wet her pants. Then, she said, "But I can't take it back."

"Then burn it, or give it to Goodwill."

Now, Gram and I were both thinking about that time. She said, "I have half a notion to go buy a black dress—just to see Richard rise up!"

We laughed and cried at the same time. That's what always saves us—remembering the funny things that Gramps said.

All the widows from our street came for calling hours. What they were wondering was who'd mow their lawns and who'd carry out their trash. I didn't feel like saying I would. Not unless they'd pay me. I guessed that Gramps's check would stop coming now. That could be a problem.

I got hugged and kissed by people I didn't know. The very worst thing about the wake was was seeing Gramps lying there in his uncomfortable suit. His shirt and tie looked like they were killing him. His hair was all slicked down, except for his cowlick.

They had a blanket of sissy satin over his feet. I wondered if they had squeezed his poor old toes into those Sunday shoes. I kept sneaking up to the foot of the casket. I tried to put my hand under the blanket to feel. But I never had a chance.

Old Mrs. Billings was blubbering like Gramps was her dearly beloved. She can manage to say something mean, even if she's just talking about the weather. And she sure does love to give advice.

"Eleanor," she said, "take my word for it. Get his things out of the house. It will break your heart every time you find something where he left it."

I thought Gram might fall apart. For a minute or two, I was really scared. Darn that woman! But she was almost the last one in line to speak to us.

People wondered if they could stop by the house after the wake. But Gram said, "No, thank you."

Pretty soon, it was over. Gram and I took time to look at the flowers. There were so many, the place looked like a garden. Gramps wouldn't have believed it. Because I was in the river all night, there was a big thing in the paper. I guess people just wanted to do something nice.

Then, Gram wanted me to go out. She wanted to be alone with Gramps for a few minutes.

I wanted to be alone with him, too. But I was afraid to say so. I wanted to ask him what it felt like to be dead.

I hated all those people staring at him. He was dressed up in clothes he hated. It wasn't fair. He couldn't stare back.

On the way home in Benson's big black car, Gram and I didn't talk. I was thinking about the wake. The worst part was that all those people we hardly knew came. But Dave didn't show up. He was Gramps's best friend.

Whenever Gram and I went out to the movies, Dave and Gramps would have a few beers at the tavern. (Gramps didn't like movies any better than he liked church.) Dave was the one who sold Gramps the camper.

That reminded me. No one had brought the camper back, either. Gram had asked them to.

If it stayed down by the river, some of the drunks that come down there might break into it.

I just realized that I was starting to think practical thoughts. "Sure sign you're pulling out of a tailspin," Gramps used to say.

When we got home, Gram put on the teakettle. We had tea and cinnamon toast.

"I've got things I want to do tonight, Mattie," she said. "You run up to bed, dear. You've had an awful couple of days. You need some rest." She gave me a hug and a squeeze. She seemed more like her old determined self.

I heard her going through closets and dresser drawers, pulling out stuff. I heard the washer and dryer going. I smelled her ironing with that nice smelling spray starch she uses.

It didn't seem strange. I've seen her work like crazy when she's upset. She'll go until she drops in her tracks.

This must be one of those times, I thought. But I couldn't sleep.

Chapter 11

Early in the morning, Gram had all of Gramps's fishing clothes ironed. They smelled sweet. They were in a basket on the kitchen table.

I remembered what old Mrs. Billings said about getting rid of Gramps's stuff. I ran upstairs and grabbed Gramps's old bedroom slippers. I put them in the back of my closet. (I still have them there, and I always will.)

I didn't think Gram would do this. It wasn't like her. Dave's not coming to the wake was bad enough. Now, Gram was getting rid of Gramps's stuff even before the funeral!

While we ate our cereal, I searched her face to figure her out.

She noticed right away. I guess she understood what I was asking with my eyes.

"Mattie, I think Richard looks so very uncomfortable in that suit. I want to go to the funeral home. I want Mr. Benson to change Richard's clothes to his grubbies."

Gram understood exactly what was bothering me.

"Yes, Gram. That's a good idea."

"It would keep the whole town talking till doomsday," she said. "So we'd better have a closed casket for the funeral. If you want to see your grandfather again, you should come with me."

She looked worried. "Nobody brought the camper back." Her lips began to quiver. She put her coffee cup down and hid her face in her apron. "I need the darn thing, but I can't bear to see it." We were both crying now.

"And where was Dave?" I bawled. "He was Gramps's best friend!"

"I was sure he'd come," Gram said. She was really crying now. I didn't know what to do. The doorbell was ringing, so I answered it.

Speak of the devil! There was Dave, all spattered with dark green paint. Some was even on his nose. He was standing there with the longhorns in his big, green hands.

I looked out to the driveway. There was the camper. It was painted dark green, just like Dave.

As soon as Gram heard Dave's voice, she came running. Dave took her in his arms. They both cried.

"I missed you so much last night," Gram said. "Where were you?"

"I've been painting the camper, Eleanor. I figured it needed that more than you needed me."

Gram looked out the door. The truck looked quite dignified.

"But, Eleanor, you don't need that thing. Don't you want the Cutlass back? It hasn't been sold yet. I'd buy the truck back for just what Richard gave me. The Cutlass is all shined up and ready to go."

"Now, Dave, that's not fair to you."

"Oh, yes, it is. And it's $3500 you can really use right now."

Gram was speechless. It was like a gift from heaven. And Dave wasn't taking no for an answer.

Dave went on, "I tried to talk Richard out of buying the camper. I ordered that crazy color so it wouldn't sell. I wanted to talk my wife into letting me keep it. But Richard walked in and insisted on taking it. And my wife was standing right there."

Gram broke down and cried. Money had been worrying her all along. Of course, she'd never tell me that.

But money wasn't the only thing. Gram's pride would break in two if she had to drive that camper. Selling it to a stranger would be disloyal to Gramps. Selling it to Dave was another matter.

"OK," she said. "But I want to pay for the paint job. That's only fair."

"No problem." Dave was going up the stairs. I hadn't noticed he had a hammer and nails with him.

"Come on up here, Mattie. Tell me where you want these longhorns on the wall in your room. We can put them close to a plug. Then you can turn the lights on if you want."

That was the first good feeling I'd had in days. I was afraid I'd never have that kind of feeling again. Dave really understood what those horns meant to me.

Now, when I feel sort of empty inside at night, I turn on the lights on the longhorns. I go to sleep watching them blink.

After Dave left, Gram said, "I can't believe all the things we were thinking about Dave. That was just half an hour ago."

Somehow, Dave's visit helped us get through that day.

Mr. Benson didn't mind changing Gramps's clothes. When he was finished, Gramps looked like his old self. I did feel his hands. They were stiff and cold. I kept wishing he'd grab my head and put it under his arm like he used to.

It was like seeing a chapter of my life close when they put the lid of the casket down.

The minister was a nice guy. He read Gramps's favorite hymn, "Father, Father, through the night." Then, he told about all the nice things Gramps did for people. "His church was the great outdoors. He was never cruel or unkind to man or beast. We could all be very proud if, at our death, this could be said of us."

I wished Gramps could have heard that.

I don't want to talk about the cemetery.

That night at home, Gram said, "A new grave looks like an open wound."

So, the next day, we dug up a lot of sod from the backyard. We planted it on Gramps's grave. We keep it planted with pansies, too.

Chapter 12

It's been over four years since all that happened. Now, I can get out the photo album and think about the good times we had.

The hardest part is having something really great happen and not being able to tell it to Gramps. I used to love to see his eyes light up. I can still hear him say, "Go get 'em, Mattie."

Every time I do something I'm really proud of, I think, that's for you, Gramps. Maybe he even knows. It's a big mystery.

There's one thing about having the worst possible thing happen and surviving it. You know you can go on. The sun does come out again. The air does smell sweet again.

Even Gram is able to joke around and be funny. That's what Gramps would have wanted for both of us.

Being loved by someone like him puts your whole soul together. And that lasts forever.